Ros Bayley's
Alliteration Raps

ACKNOWLEDGEMENTS

Written by: Ros Bayley

Illustrated by: Peter Scott

Produced by: Lynda Lawrence.

Published by: Lawrence Educational Ltd.
                   Unit 21, Brookvale Trading Estate,
                   Birmingham B6 7AQ

          ©   Lawrence Educational 2009

ISBN: 978-1-903670-80-4

W0007885

2

CONTENTS

What is alliteration?

Alliteration is the repetition of the same sounds or the same kind of sounds at the beginning of words or in stressed syllables, as in *'Peter Piper picked a peck of pickled peppers.'*

It is also known as 'head rhyme' or 'initial rhyme' and usually involves the repetition of consonant sounds in two or more neighbouring words.

INTRODUCTION

The importance of alliteration to children's literacy development cannot be overstated. When they sing or say rhymes and jingles with alliterative lines their ears become tuned to the relationships between the sound structures of words, and this is extremely important to later work in phonics.

Ultimately children need to be able to hear initial phonemes in isolation and in order to do this they need plenty of experience of hearing words that begin with the same sound. The rhymes in this book are designed to extend their repertoire of rhymes and can be used in any way that you want to use them. Broadly speaking they are ordered from the simple to the more complex but they can be used in whatever order is most appropriate for your children.

Once the children are familiar with the rhymes they can innovate on them and this will provide a wealth of opportunities for discussion about words and language and support vocabulary development. In some cases ideas for innovation are included in the text and words that can be changed appear in italics. However, these are only suggestions and you will probably find that the children will come up with even more ideas for having fun with the language in the book. You will probably also find that they will begin to make up their own alliterative rhymes. I hope this little rap book is a useful addition to your collection of alliterative material!

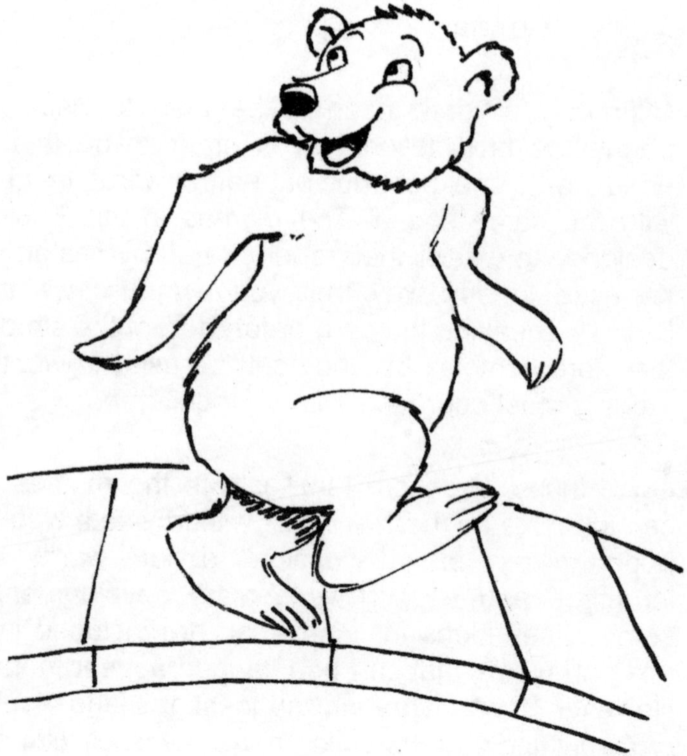

The Big Brown Bear

(This rhyme can be sung to the tune of 'Here we go Round the Mulberry Bush')

The big brown bear bounced over the bridge
Over the bridge, over the bridge
The big brown bear bounced over the bridge
To see what he could see.
He saw a snake that slithered and slid
Slithered and slid, slithered and slid
He saw a snake that slithered and slid
That's what he did see!

The big brown bear bounced over the bridge
Over the bridge, over the bridge
The big brown bear bounced over the bridge
To see what he could see.
He saw a crow that cackled and cawed
Cackled and cawed, cackled and cawed
He saw a crow that cackled and cawed
That's what he did see!

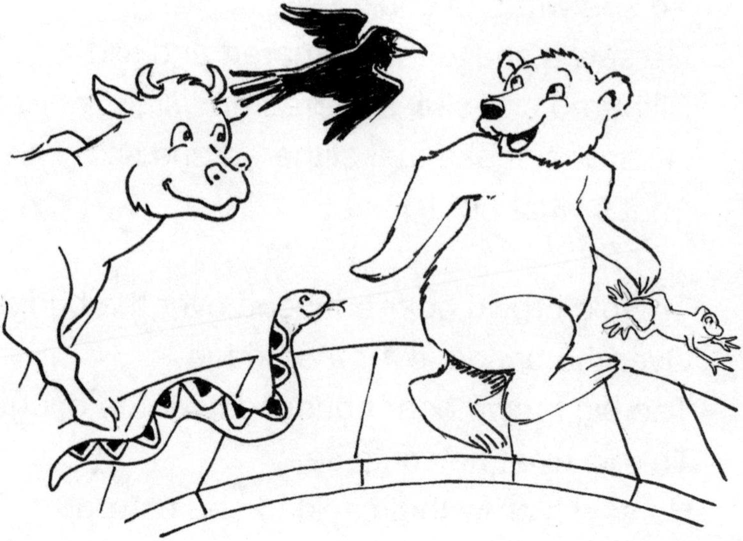

The big brown bear bounced over the bridge
Over the bridge, over the bridge
The big brown bear bounced over the bridge
To see what he could see.
He saw a frog who was frightened of fire
Frightened of fire, frightened of fire
He saw a frog who was frightened of fire
That's what he did see!

The big brown bear bounced over the bridge
Over the bridge, over the bridge
The big brown bear bounced over the bridge
To see what he could see.
He saw a cow that was crunching on corn
Crunching on corn, crunching on corn
He saw a crow that was crunching on corn
That's what he did see!

The big brown bear bounced back over the
bridge
Over the bridge, over the bridge
The big brown bear bounced back over the
bridge
He said, 'look they're all following me!'

Wendy Wobble

(This can be sung to the tune of Frere Jacques)

Wendy Wobble, Wendy Wobble,

Wants white wool.

Wants white wool.

Wendy will you wash wool?

Wendy will you wash wool?

Wash white wool, wash white wool.

Going to the Shops

I went to the shops

'Cause I wanted to get

Some food to eat for tea.

I bought *carrots* and *cabbages,*

cakes and *cream.*

I said, 'That will do for me!'

Once the children know the rhyme, encourage them to change the words in italics for foods beginning with a different sound.

Snakes, Spiders, Slugs and Snails

(This can be sung to the tune of 'Heads, Shoulders, Knees and Toes')

Snakes, spiders, slugs and snails,
slugs and snails.

Snakes, spiders, slugs and snails,
slugs and snails.

And wasps and wolves and worms
and whales,

Snakes, spiders, slugs and snails,
slugs and snails.

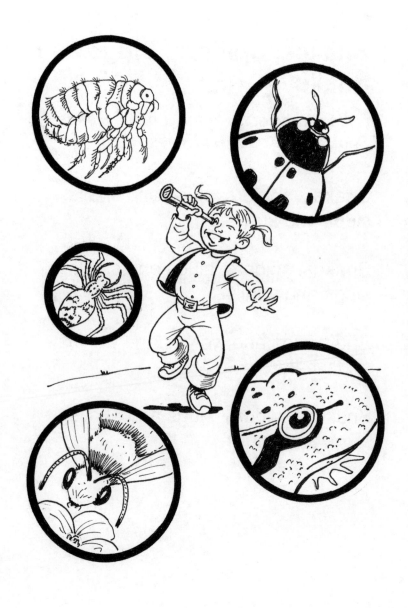

Through my Telescope

I looked through my telescope
What did I see?
I saw lots of little ladybirds
And one fat flea!
I looked through my telescope
What did I see?
I saw six small spiders
And a big bumble bee!
I looked through my telescope
What did I see?
I saw five fat frogs
All looking at me!
I looked through my telescope
What did I see?
I saw a big bouncing baby
On his granny's knee!
I looked through my telescope
What did I see?
I saw a dozen dirty dogs
All going for a wee!

The Beach

I went to the beach
One sunny day
To see what I could spy
I saw *sand* and *sea* and *sailing ships*
And the sun so high in the sky.

Once the children know the rhyme, encourage them to change the words in italics for foods beginning with a different sound.

In the Street

As I was walking down the street
This is who I chanced too meet:
I saw fearless fire fighters
And big brave boy bikers
A merry muscle man
And a vampire in a van
Some lively little ladies
And a big bouncing baby
A leopard in a lorry
And a dainty dancing dolly
When **you** walk down the street
I wonder who **you** will meet.

Knock, Knock!

Knock, knock on my door
One knock and then one more
A voice said, 'Open if you dare!'
And this is what was standing there:
A *greedy great* gibbon
In a *gold* and *green* ribbon.
Some *pretty pink* poodles
Doing *drawings* and doodles
A *frightened fat* frog
Frying food in the fog
Witches and wizards
Ladybirds and lizards
Some *monkeys* and moles
And *hamsters* in holes
Knock, knock who's there?
Open up if you dare!

Once the children are familiar with the rhyme, encourage them to change the words in italics for words beginning with the same sound.

Names

Billy Bates blew big brown bubbles in the big blue bath.

Patsy Perkins planted plums in pairs in Pershore Park.

Shirley Sage smelt savoury snacks in Samuel Sutton's shop.

Malcolm Moore hit Molly Mann with Mrs. Mason's mop.

Kelvin Kent kept kittens in his cousin Katy's cupboard.

Hannah Holland had a hair slide from Hermione Hubbard.

Daniel Dunn did dire drawings of Doctor Drabble dancing.

Peter Pine poured perfume on a pony that was prancing.

The Woods

If you go down to the woods at night

You'll see some things that will give you a fright

'Cause standing there behind the trees

Are things to scare both you and me!

Wolves and wizards, wasps and worms

Snakes so slithery, they make you squirm

Forest frogs and frightening foxes

Badgers and beetles that bounce out of boxes

Owls and ogres and an octopus

Frantic fire-eaters making a fuss

So unless you like to be given a fright

Do **not** go down to the woods at night!

The Fair

One night at the fair

What do **you** think was there?

There was a blue balloon and a sparkling spoon

Two tubby teddies and a monster moon

Three thin thrushes and rollercoaster ride

Four fat fairies all wiggling and wide

Five fat fish and a dormouse in a dish

Six sad sardines and a witch with a wish

Seven short snakes and a white wagon wheel

Eight electric eels and a marmalade meal

Nine nice nectarines and a peach and a pear

Ten tall tents and a ballerina bear

That's just some of the things that were there!

And all I could do was stand and stare!

The Dream

I had a dream so very weird

Of Batman with a big black beard

Where doggies danced with dragonflies

And peacocks pecked at pizza pies

Where cats were kissing kangaroos

And slithery snakes slid into my shoes

Where parrots paraded in the park

And dragons were drumming in the dark

Where sheep in shorts were being sheared

And hunting horns could hardly be heard

Where rabbits were red and ran round in rings

And sharks and sheepdogs could shout and sing

Where a tiger tumbled from a tall trapeze

And snails and snakes they made me sneeze

I had this dream, it was not good

I would forget it if I could!

The Zoo

I went to the zoo and I looked around

There were lots of sights and lots of sounds

There were mischievous monkeys making merry

Blue budgies biting berries

Greedy gorillas that grumbled and groaned

Mad meerkats that met and moaned

Hungry horses huddled round hay

Dusty ducks who drank all day

I went to the zoo and I looked around

And these were some of the things I found.

Fruits

Merry Mandy Marriott munched a mouldy melon.

Lazy Larry Lancelot licked a little lemon
Pretty Polly Peterson plucked a purple plum.

Ronnie Richard-Robinson ate raspberries with rum.

Dainty Dolly Donaldson ate damsons for a dare.

Perky Pauline Peterson picked a polished pear.

Paunchy Pirate Pedro poured popcorn on a peach.

Blooming Betty Bailey ate bananas on Bournemouth beach!

We hope you have enjoyed our '**Alliteration**' Raps.

Other books in the same series are:

Ros Bayley's **Action Raps**	978-1-903670-42-2
Ros Bayley's **Action Raps 2**	978-1-903670-55-2
Ros Bayley's **Animal Raps**	978-1-903670-38-5
Ros Bayley's **Beanbag Raps**	978-1-903670-43-9
Ros Bayley's **Creepy Crawly**	978-1-903670-52-1
Ros Bayley's **Five Senses Raps**	978-1-903670-59-0
Ros Bayley's **Noisy Raps**	978-1-903670-44-6
Ros Bayley's **Sticks, Plates**	978-1-903670-51-4
Ros Bayley's **Mouse Raps**	978-1-903670-66-8
Ros Bayley's **Monkey Raps**	978-1-903670-78-1

Additional rhymes and further guidance on developing children's beat competency can be found in our '**Helping Young Children with Steady Beat**' publication.

ISBN: 978-1-903670-26-2

Available to purchase with this book is a small cuddly toy called **BEAT BABY,** who can be used at the beginning and end of sessions to help focus the children and to bring emotional engagement to the whole process.

For further details of these and our many other publications, visit our website:

www.educationalpublications.com